D0771409

A. A. Livingston • Illustrated by Joey Chou

B. Bear and Lolly

Catch That Cookie!

HARPER
An Imprint of HarperCollinsPublishers

For my dad, with love.
—A.A.L.

To my mother, and to all
the mama bears in the world.
—J.C.

B. Bear and Lolly: Catch That Cookie!

For information address HarperCollins Children's Books, a division of HarperCollins Publishers, 195 Broadway, New York, NY 10007.
www.harpercollinschildrens.com

Library of Congress Cataloging-in-Publication Data
Livingston, A. A.
B. Bear and Lolly : catch that cookie! / A. A. Livingston ; Illustrated by Joey Chou. — First Edition.
pages cm
Summary: Best friends B. Bear and Lolly are working on their invention, a Porridge Perfecter, when the Gingerbread Man wrecks the machine and keeps running without apologizing or offering to help.
ISBN 978-0-06-219791-7 (hardcover bdg.)
[1. Inventions—Fiction. 2. Best friends—Fiction. 3. Friendship—Fiction. 4. Cookies—Fiction. 5. Characters in literature—Fiction. 6. Bears—Fiction.] I. Chou, Joey, illustrator. II. Title. III. Title: Catch that cookie!
PZ7.L755.Baat 2014 2013032815
[E]—dc23 CIP
AC

The artist used Adobe Illustrator to create the digital illustrations for this book.
Typography by Martha Rago.
15 16 17 18 19 SCP 10 9 8 7 6 5 4 3 2 1
❖
First Edition

B.Bear and Lolly were the best of friends. And why not? They liked the same porridge, the same chair, and the same comfy bed.

One day, B. Bear and Lolly were hard at work on a new invention: the Porridge Perfecter.

Unfortunately, the porridge was anything but perfect.

Too thick.

Too slick.

Too lumpy.

Too jumpy.
Too sticky.
TOO
ICKY!
They were about
to try again when . . .

. . . the Gingerbread Man
burst into the clearing
and ran right through
their invention.

The Porridge Perfecter
teetered . . .

it tottered . . .

and it
toppled over!

CRASH!

B. Bear tried not to cry. "The Gingerbread Man didn't even say he was sorry. He just ran off."

Lolly wasn't sad—she was mad. "*And* he didn't stay to help clean up his mess! Let's go get him!"

The chase was on!

But they just couldn't catch that cookie.

The Gingerbread Man looked back and sang:

"Run, run, as fast as you can.
You can't catch me—
I'm the Gingerbread Man!"

"Ooh!" shouted Lolly.
"I just want to crumble
that cookie!"

B. Bear had a plan. He made a map, rigged a net, and was ready to snatch his catch! When the Gingerbread Man zoomed by, B. Bear pulled the rope . . .

PLAN
A

. . . and missed.

Lolly giggled. “Close, but no cookie!”

It was time for Lolly's plan. She made a scary mask to stop the Gingerbread Man in his tracks.

When the Gingerbread Man ran by, she jumped out and yelled,

"BOO!"

But the Gingerbread Man was *so* scared, he ran away even faster than before!

"Oh, golly, Lolly!" said B. Bear. "We'll never catch the Gingerbread Man. He's just too fast!"

Back at the clearing, B. Bear's stomach gurgled and growled.

"Porridge! That's it!" he said.

The two friends set a perfect porridge trap. When the Gingerbread Man rounded a corner,

he slipped . . .

he slid . . .

and he was stuck!

“Yay!” cheered Lolly. “We finally caught you!”

The Gingerbread Man trembled like a leaf. “Don’t eat me!”

“We’re not going to *eat* you,” explained B. Bear. “We *need* you.”

“Whew! I’m so glad,” said the Gingerbread Man. “Wait . . . need me for what?”

“We’ll show you,” said Lolly.

"Goodness gumdrops!" said the Gingerbread Man when he saw the giant mess. "I'm so sorry! How about if I help you put it back together?"

"That's *exactly* what we were thinking," said Lolly.

When they were done rebuilding the Porridge Perfecter, the machine looked great.

"There's only one problem," said B. Bear. "We *still* can't make perfect porridge."

The Gingerbread Man offered to help. “It’s the least I can do.”

He checked the water. He checked the oats.

“Aha!” he said finally. “There’s no spoon! You need to keep the porridge moving—just like me!”

So he spun it . . .

he swirled it . . .

and he stirred it up.

He even thought of a new song:

"Stir, stir, as fast as I can.
Who's making porridge?
The Gingerbread Man!"

Soon the new friends shared their first porridge together. It tasted . . .

JUST RIGHT!